DATE DUE

JE 27 '85	JY 15 '04		
JE 13 '87	AG 10 '04		
JY 30 '87	JA 17 '07		
	FE 03		
JY 5 '89			
JY 17 '90			
JE 24 '91			
SE 9 '91			
MAR 28 '96			
JUN 27 '96			
JUL 08 '96			
DEC 27 '96			
JUL 14 '97			
JL 25 '97			
AUG 1 2 '98			
OCT 1 4 '98			
JY 0 3 '02			

NOBODY SCARES a PORCUPINE

NOBODY SCARES a PORCUPINE

by JEAN HORTON BERG

Illustrated by
ROBERT L. JEFFERSON

THE WESTMINSTER PRESS
Philadelphia

STANDARD BOOK NO. 664-32438-X
LIBRARY OF CONGRESS CATALOG CARD NO. 69-12906

PUBLISHED BY THE WESTMINSTER PRESS ®
PHILADELPHIA, PENNSYLVANIA
PRINTED IN THE UNITED STATES OF AMERICA

For Jeanie,
who is brave

Deep within the darkness of the old
hollow log Little Porcupine stretched himself
and yawned *hoooooooooooo-hummmmmmmmm.*

"I need to do something," he said. "What
is it I need to do?"

He peered out the doorway. The sun was climbing high in the sky.

Little Porcupine blinked and started to yawn again.

Hooooooo— But his jaws snapped shut in the middle of the yawn.

"What I need is to get something to eat," he said. "I'm hungry!"

He climbed up into a young maple tree,
and stuffed himself with tender maple bark
and tasty maple leaves.

After while Little Porcupine ambled down the woodland path. He came upon a box with some salt spilling out.

"Lucky for me I didn't stuff too much," he said. "I have just enough room left for this much salt. Just exactly."

But the box had a man-smell. The smell wasn't very strong, but it was worrisome. The smell made Little Porcupine's quills stand up. The smell made his tail quiver. The smell made him look up the path and down the path to be sure no two-legged creature was near.

As far as he could see, nothing was moving.
So Little Porcupine licked up the last lickerish
grain of salt and started down the path again.

He went a very little way when he smelled the man-smell even stronger. The smell grew stronger and sharper with every step he took. So Little Porcupine stood still.

"My stars," he said. "Men must be coming this way. And fast."

Suddenly he saw them. The men walked tall on their two legs. They walked straight down the path toward Little Porcupine. Little Porcupine stood still and watched them coming.

"Men won't touch me," he said. "Not if they really know about porcupines, they won't. NOBODY EVER SCARES A PORCUPINE.

"But just in case they haven't heard about porcupines—" He climbed quietly and quickly up into the sheltering branches of another little maple tree.

Little Porcupine lay very still along a branch and watched the men walk past the tree. He watched while they walked on down the path. He stayed there, gnawing the bark absentmindedly, until they were out of sight.

Little Porcupine was about to climb down out of the tree when he saw something moving on the ground below.

Under the tree, Tiny Mouse crouched beside the woodland path. He was stuffing himself with seeds from the sweet wild grass. Every little while Tiny Mouse stopped to brush the husks from his whiskers and to snuff the air.

"There isn't any smell of danger, or Tiny Mouse wouldn't be there," thought Little Porcupine.

But, what was that?

Little Squirrel was creeping quietly up behind Tiny Mouse.

"Boo!" said Little Squirrel.
"EEEEEEEEEEEEEEEEEEEEEEEE!"
Tiny Mouse jumped about a foot straight up into the air. When he landed on his feet, he scampered into the tall grass.

Little Squirrel laughed and laughed.
"Come on out," he said. "I didn't mean to scare you that much."

Tiny Mouse crept timidly out into the path again. His whiskers jiggled nervously.

"I can't help being scared," he said. "Anybody can scare a mouse. Lots of animals like to eat mice. Skunks and weasels and foxes would eat me if they could catch me. I have to be careful every minute I'm out of my nest."

"Well, you can be careful without falling apart," said Little Squirrel. "Be brave like me."

"Little Squirrel is exactly right," thought Little Porcupine. "Just exactly." He was about to call out to Little Squirrel and tell him so when he saw something.

Little Muskrat was creeping quietly up behind Little Squirrel.

"Boo!" said Little Muskrat.

"CHEEEEEEEEEEEEEEEEEEEE!"

Little Squirrel jumped about three feet straight up into the air. When he landed on his feet he scampered up into the nearest tree.

Little Muskrat laughed and laughed.

"Come on down," he said. "I didn't mean to scare you that much."

"Just how much did you mean to scare me?" said Little Squirrel crossly.

Little Squirrel walked down the tree headfirst, flapping his tail. He looked carefully to one side, then to the other. Then he sat down on the path again.

"I thought you were a dog," he said. "Dogs have been coming deeper and deeper into the forest lately. A dog nearly caught me the other day."

"Of course you have to watch out for dogs," agreed Little Muskrat. "But you don't have to fall apart whenever you hear a noise. Be brave like me."

"He's right," thought Little Porcupine.
"Just exactly right. I'm going to tell him so."

But just then he saw Little Beaver creeping up behind Little Muskrat.

Little Beaver didn't make a sound.

Then— "BOOOOOOOOO!" said Little Beaver.

"AAAAAAAAAAAAAAAAAAAAAAAAH!"

Little Muskrat jumped about four feet straight up into the air. He had hardly landed on his feet when he scrambled down the river bank.

Little Beaver laughed and laughed.
"Come on up," he said. "I didn't think you
were scared of anything. Didn't I hear you
tell Little Squirrel to be brave like you?"

"Hardly anybody scares a muskrat," said Little Muskrat huffily. He climbed up the river bank and sat dripping on the path. "I'm only scared of scary things, like wolves and men and dogs."

"They're scary, all right," said Little Beaver. "But most of the time you can hear them or smell them long before they are anywhere near. So you don't have to fall apart. Be brave like me."

"He's so right," thought Little Porcupine. "Little Beaver is exactly right. No make-believe scare would ever scare him. He's really brave!"

Quickly and quietly Little Porcupine climbed down from the maple tree and hurried over to Little Beaver.

"YOU'RE RIGHT!" said Little Porcupine right in Little Beaver's ear.

"AAAAAAAAAAAAAAAAAAAAAAAAAAH!"

Little Beaver jumped about five feet straight up into the air.

He had hardly landed on his feet when he slithered down the river bank.

Little Porcupine felt awful. "Come on back up," he called. "I didn't think *you'd* be scared."

Little Beaver climbed wetly up the river bank.

"I wasn't really scared," he said. "Nobody ever scares a beaver—very much. But when—"

"Hsssst! What's that?" said Little Squirrel.
Everybody pricked up his ears.

Off in the distance there was a frightening noise. The noise came closer and closer.

"Those are dogs barking," cried Little Muskrat. "And they're coming this way."

"There might be men with them," muttered Little Beaver. "There usually are."

Whish! Tiny Mouse whisked into the tall grass.

Whoosh! Little Squirrel scampered up a tree.

Swish! Little Muskrat tumbled down the river bank into Deep River.

Swoosh! Little Beaver tumbled after him.

Little Porcupine listened a minute. He lifted his head and snuffed the air. "Yep, they're dogs, all right," he said. Then he ambled over to the spreading roots of an old oak tree and curled up into a little ball.

"Climb up here with me, Little Porcupine," chattered Little Squirrel from a branch high in the tree.

"Crawl in here with me, Little Porcupine," squeaked Tiny Mouse from a hollow in the tall grass.

"Slide down here with us, Little Porcupine," yelped Little Muskrat and Little Beaver. Only their heads were sticking out of Deep River.

Bow-ow-ow-ow-ow!   The hounds were coming closer and closer.

Little Porcupine didn't pay any attention to any of them—not to Tiny Mouse, not to Little Squirrel, not to Little Muskrat, and not to Little Beaver. He didn't pay any attention to the baying of the hounds. Nobody ever scares a porcupine.

ZZZZZZZZZZZZZZZZZZZZZZZZZZZZZ!

Little Porcupine was snoring.

Down the woodland path raced the
hounds. The first hound caught sight of Little
Porcupine.

"Hey, fellows," he howled. "Here's something. Come on over here."

Tiny Mouse was so scared he nearly fell down a mole hole.

Little Squirrel was so scared he nearly fell out of the oak tree.

Little Muskrat was so scared he stepped on Little Beaver's head.

Little Beaver was so scared he dived straight down and barely escaped getting stuck in the mud at the bottom of Deep River.

Little Porcupine yawned a wide yawn. *HOOOOOOOO-HUMMMMMMMM,* and he began to snore again.

Nobody ever scared a porcupine. *ZZZZZZZZZZZZZZZZZZZZZZZZZZZZ!*

The first hound skidded to a stop beside Little Porcupine.

He was just about to jump on Little Porcupine when he took a good look at him.

"WOOF!" the hound woofed in surprise. Then he jumped about six feet straight up into the air. When he landed on his feet he turned around and started running right back in the direction he came from.

"This way, boys," he yelped. "Come this way. Don't go near that pesky pricker fellow!"

"Are you scared of a little animal like that?" howled one of the hounds.

The first hound didn't stop running.

"I'm not scared, friend," he bawled back over his shoulder. "I just know about porcupines. Don't touch that fellow if you don't want your nose and paws full of prickery quills. It happened to me once. But never again!"

For a few minutes the rest of the dogs pawed the ground uncertainly. Then one hound yelped, "I'm not scared of an animal that is no bigger than I am."

Snarling fiercely, the hound pranced over and poked Little Porcupine with his paw.

Yi-yi-yi-yi-yi-yi-yi-yi-yi! The hound dog's snarl turned into a howl of pain. He galloped off on three legs.

The rest of the pack milled around. They snuffed at Little Porcupine. They snarled and growled—but they did not get too close. Pretty soon all the hound dogs turned around and trotted off.

"I could have told him," said one of the
older dogs. "My father ran into a porcupine
once. You should have seen him. It took our
master three days to get all the prickery quills
out of his paws and his nose. He never did
get all of them out."

Tiny Mouse crept out from the tall grass.

"My, you were brave, Little Porcupine," he said.

Little Squirrel scampered down the tree trunk headfirst.

"My, my, you were brave, Little Porcupine," he said.

Little Muskrat and Little Beaver scrambled up the river bank.

"My, my, my, you were brave, Little Porcupine," they said.

Little Porcupine yawned and stretched. "I wasn't really so brave," he said. "Nobody scares a porcupine. I knew the dogs wouldn't hurt me—not if they knew what a porcupine is. Hardly anybody that knows about porcupines would touch one. And there wasn't a bit of man-smell in the air.

"Tiny Mouse is brave, though. He's afraid of lots of things. But he comes out into the world anyway. Little Squirrel is brave, too. He's afraid of dogs, but he comes out into the world anyway. Little Muskrat and Little Beaver are brave. They're afraid of wolves and dogs and men. But that doesn't keep them from coming out into the world."

"My stars! Aren't you ever scared of anybody?" Little Squirrel asked admiringly. "Never *ever?*"

Little Porcupine cleared his throat. "Well, hardly ever." He looked embarrassed. "If you really want to know," he said, "there's only one thing that scares me. When I curl up to take a nap, I'm always just a little bit scared that some of my own sharp quills will stick me."

Little Squirrel puffed out his cheeks and
swished his tail up and down.

"That's the silliest thing I ever heard,"
he chattered.

Little Muskrat jumped up and down and laughed. "It is silly, isn't it?"

Little Beaver slapped the ground with his flat tail and giggled.

"It's the silliest thing I ever heard of," he said. "It's quite right to be scared of scary things, but you're just plain *silly*, Little Porcupine."

"He's silly, all right," the others snickered. "Silly-billy Porcupine!"

"Wait!" Tiny Mouse hopped up and down, squeaking as loud as he could. "Wait! *Wait!* WAIT! Listen! *Listen!* LISTEN!"

The others finally stopped snickering. Tiny Mouse stood tall on his hind legs.

"Brave is doing what you ought to do, even when you're scared—that's what brave is," said Tiny Mouse.

The little animals looked at each other.

"Then you are brave, Tiny Mouse, when you come out of your nest," said Little Squirrel.

"Then you are brave, Little Squirrel, when you come out of your tree," said Little Muskrat.

"And you are brave, Little Beaver, when you come up the river bank," said Tiny Mouse.

But Little Porcupine was curling himself
up into a ball once more. And all he said was
"ZZZZZZZZZZZZZZZZZZZZZZZZZZZZZZZZZZ!"